By Richard Kelso
Illustrated by Lane Gregory

Chapter 1 . . . . . Page 2
Chapter 2 . . . . Page 18

Copyright © 2000 Metropolitan Teaching and Learning Company.
Published by Metropolitan Teaching and Learning Company.
Printed in the United States of America.
All rights reserved. No part of this publication may be reproduced or utilized in any form or by any means, electronic or mechanical, including photocopying, recording, or by any information storage or retrieval system without permission in writing from the publisher. For information regarding permission, write to Metropolitan Teaching and Learning Company, 33 Irving Place, New York, NY 10003.

ISBN 1-58120-032-3

2 3 4 5 6 7 8 9 CL 02 01 00

Ben said, "Our pets have not been to school before.
This will be a lot of fun.
What will Boo do at the pet show?"

Marta said, "Tell me what your hermit crab will do.
It can't jump or sit up."

Jed said, "Who knows what my crab will do?
But I have some time.
I will have to see."

Jed said, "The pet show is in two days. Ben and Marta will take their pets. What can my crab do in the show?"

Grandmother said, "We don't have a hat for the crab. We don't have a little bow. What can we put on top of the shell?"

Jed said, "Dan gave me this little fake frog.
We can put it on top of the shell.
This fake frog can ride on top."

Grandmother said, "You are all set for the pet show.
You can show your crab to the kids.
You can show them what it can do."

Chapter 2: Go, Crab! Go!

Jed said, "This will be a good show.
I see Marta and Boo.
Marta said Boo can jump very well."

Dan said, "It is time for the pet show.
You will see many pets.
You will get to know all of them."

Marta said, "They can glide from side to side!
That frog and crab are very good!
Go, crab! Go!"

Ben said, "You and your crab were a big hit!"

Jed said, "I am very glad about that. We all have pets we can brag about."